KB260667

저자 근영

백한이 시집
A Collection of H. Y. Baek's Poems

고 려 달 빛

The Moon Light of Corea

Published HANNURY MEDIA

CONTENTS 차 례

CONTENTS

차 례

CONTENTS 차 례

CONTENTS 차 례

CONTENTS 차 례

+-=0

목동교가 막힌 것은 너 때문이다
말도 안돼 9시 50분 합승손님
가능성에 불가능이 앞서 절박한 5분
시장 로터리 기적 같은 것이 일어나
낭패구멍에 뚫린 굴을 헤집고 승차 4분 전에
8차선 중앙에서 뛰어내려 지하도 계단
계단 에스컬레이터 계단 계단 에스컬레이터
출발과 동시 승차의 시차는 -+=0였다

심장의 피스톤 속력은 절정을 넘고
미끄러지듯 스쳐가는 침목, 침목, 침목
북해 탄광선로에 깔린 동태, 동태, 시체
사할린 북변 철로 밑 조선인의 조선인의
비명이 그친 침목, 침목, 침목의 환영이
차창에 각인되어 따라온다

돌아본 할머니 초점 잃은 눈동자에
한을 비집고 솟구치는 긴 한숨
저 멀리 통절되는 물안개 속으로
"어혀영차 어허야" 장송가 띄운다

수없이 포개져 쌓여 있는 침목
백지 위에 수많은 침목을 그리다가 멎은 눈에
열네 살 이마 아래 미간 아래 그 아래
시작과 끝의 시차는 +-=0

금강교 아래 나성리 우회전 돌아
살구 묘목밭 뒤 공원묘원
5,000의 영혼은 편히 잠들어 있을까
심심 구릉에 금잔디, 잔디, 잔디
하반세기 또한 반세기 접어들어도
원색으로 일어서지 못하는 기차길
통한의 침목 침목은 너 때문이다
햇님 따라 금강은 유유히 흐르고
바람은 오늘따라 말이 없다

+−=0

It is you who caused the traffic at Mokdong Bridge
It's ridiculous to take a subway in five minutes,
Before you take a taxi at 9:50,
Making a way at the crowded market rotary,
Taking escalator and stepping down,
Finally getting on the subway.
The time difference between departure
And getting on it was -+=0.

The piston speed of heart is over the climax;
Rail ties are passing by.
Alongside the North Sea coal mines
Are scattered corpses like frozen pollack.
Just like phantoms those cries of Chosun people
Under the train ties are followed on the train windows.

Heavy sighs of Grandma which comes from the deep sorrow
Gathers on her pointless eyes;
An elegy is floating over the wet fog, Ah! Ah!
Hundreds of rail ties are piled;
A girl stops drawing those ties on her white paper;
On her eyebrow the time difference is printed: +-=0.

Next to Nasung-ri under Kumgang Bridge
Lies a cemetery by the apricot hills;

Are those souls over fifty hundreds resting peacefully?
The rail roads are not found as their original after half-
century;
The rail ties are filled with sorrow.
Today Kumkang River is flowing peacefully;
The wind is sleeping.

비치 가든

Costa 호텔 옥상에 옥황상제가 춤을 추고
까마득한 창문에 인간 그림자 어른거린다
쏟아지는 아카풀코 햇살이 삼켜 버려
한 점 흠 찾을 길 없는 쪽빛 하늘
청록의 정액을 휘감고 춤추는 야자수에
미련의 추억을 심고 있는 보헤미안
망중한 눈동자에 비키니 살결이 꿈결같다
저 멀리 태평양 해원에서
넘실거리며 밀려오는 행복한 애수는
가슴 깊이 물 타오르는 사랑의 미로
그 아름다움에 취해 정중동
허공을 유영하는 천사가 된다.

Beach Garden

On the roof of Cosca Hotel is dancing
The highest of the heavenly gods;
The shadows of walking men in the hall
Are screened into the small windows.
Pretty far the deep-violet blue sky is so crystal clear
After the pouring Acapulco sunshine gulp down the dirts in
the sky.
Under the dancing palm trees
A bohemian carries his thoughts back to the past;
Into his dreamy eyes comes the beauties dressed in bikini.
As a happy pathos is rolling over the father Pacific Ocean,
So a passionate love is burning his heart.
He becomes an angel floating over the sky
Intoxicated with his beautiful love.

바히아 데 아카풀코만 파도

잘은 모르기에 어렴풋이 생각나면서
알 듯 모를 듯 엷은 물안개 속에
그것이 진한 그리움이란 미처 몰랐지
잡힐 것만 같이 가까이 있는 한 영혼의 뜰
다소곳 꽃길이 꿈결같기에
잠 못 이루는 파도소리가 애달프다
알 것만 같운 그 생각을 사랑하기에
가슴 뿌듯 밀려오는 행복에 술 취해 울고
알 것만 같은 내 마음에 다짐도 한다
나의 길은 시인의 길 그 삶은 시인 것을
걸으며 일하고 일하며 걷는 옥타비오
내 가슴에 출렁이는 아카풀코 파도여
Bahia De Acapulco만 언제 먼동 트려나
끓는 열정 억누른 채 놓쳐 버린 순간들
행복한 그리움만 살아서 숨쉰다
가슴이 쓰리도록 잠 못 드는 이 밤에
아카풀코 아카풀코 옥타비오 파도
한 폭의 그림으로 쉼없이 색칠한다

Bahia De Acapulco Bay Waves

I couldn't recognize that it was an irresistible yearning
Before I see it through the misty wet fog.
Dreamy is the flowery road in a soul's yard;
The roaring waves are restless even at night.
Cherishing my dream I often cry in happiness;
I bet my way is that of poet,
And my life is a poem itself.
I am walking and working Octavio.
Oh, Acapulco waves surging into my mind!
When can I meet with sunset in Bahia De Acapulco Bay?
I miss the missing moments full of passions;
Only happy longings breathe in my heart.
Tonight I cannot sleep with sore heart;
Acapulco, Acapulco Octavio waves are coloring
A beautiful picture continuously.

자전구사색
— 새 천년 새 해 새 아침 거짓말

탄생은 보통사람 1, 2, 3, 4……
저마다 같은 길을 내달린다
경주하듯 같은 길을 달려간다
저마다 외장은 짙어가고
달리는 위력 따라 덧칠한다
미친 듯이 미친 듯이 미친다……

한 인간이 미치면 절대 신은 하나요
두 인간이 미치면 절대 신은 둘이요
세 인간이 미치면 절대 신은 셋이요
네 인간이 미치면 절대 신은 넷이요……
　한 사람이 새 아침 해 하나 맞이하오
　두 사람이 새 아침 해 하나 맞이하오
　세 사람이 새 아침 해 하나 맞이하오
　제 사람이 새 아침 해 하나 맞이하오……
　　한 인간은 드디어 신이 된다
　　두 인간은 드디어 절대 신이 된다
　　세 인간은 드디어 절대 신이 된다
　　네 인간은 드디어 전능한 사람이 된다……
그 거짓새 한 마리 두 마리, 세, 네 마리……

새 천년 새 아침에 날려 보내면
태양은 그 한 목숨 끝날 때까지
스스로의 가슴 속에 영원히 살아
새 천년 새 해 새 아침 찾지 않는다

Ode to the Rotating Earth
— A new lie on the new morn in the New Year's Day, New Millenium

Babies are born one by one; 1,2,3,4.....
peoples move on the one way.
As though they run a race.
Each has a dense make-up and run fast;
They run with madness......

If one man is mad, the almighty god is one;
If two men are mad, the almighty god becomes two;
If three men are mad, the almighty god becomes three;
If four men are mad, the almighty god becomes fore....

One man greets the new sun on the New Year's Day;
Two men greet the new sun on the New Year's Day;
Three men greet the new sun on the New Year's Day;
Four men greet the new sun on the New Year's Day;

At last one man becomes a god;
At last two men become an almighty God;
At last three men become an almighty God;
At last four men become an almighty God;

If we fly those birds on the new morn in a new millenium,
All the birds tell a lie one by one;
Each bird lives in our hearts,
And the sun does not seek for the new morning
On the New Year's Day in a new millenium
Until the end of its life.

자전구 사색
― 공전

지구가 지금 막 떠오르고 있다
시뻘겋게 달구어진 얼굴을 감추며
정동진역에서 떠오르고 있다
차디차게 식어가는
지평선을 껴안고 하얀 달이 돌고 있다
기꺼이 식어 버리고 말 사랑과 연민으로
그래도 못 잊어 못 잊는다며
끊임없이 따라 돌고 있다
종말이 올 때까지라도
영원을 약속이라도 하는 듯
25시 지금 나는 하늘에 머물고 있다
아직은 지구의 몸부림 지켜보면서
낮달은 그냥 거기에 있다

Ode to the Rotating Earth
— The Earth' s Revolution

The Earth is rising up;
Rising up with its red face
Over Jungdongjin station.
The white moon turns round and round
Cherishing the horizon with its red face,
As if it could not forget its love and yearning
Which will be cooled soon.
I stay in heaven at twenty-five o' clock
As if I could secure the eternity
Till the death of the Earth.
The day-moon stays still there
Watching the Earth' s struggling.

시선이 되어(안브라지미르)

엄마야—
당신은 무슨 죄를 지었길래
구천을 울리는 여린 아이의 표정으로
안 브라지미르 화필은 깊은 한의 샘을 퍼내고 있다
무엇이 우리를 불모의 소금땅으로 내몰았을까
홍경래란, 한러수교, 러일전쟁, 한일합방,
볼셰비키혁명, 3.1 운동 그것보다는
석빙고에 위선과 권위의 사과를 저장해 두고
즐기는 탐관오리 발씻은 큰 강물 흐름 속에
진실 배반 제단 위 기복 비는 인심 때문이어라
어두움이 가련함을 숨겨줄 수 있다면야
뽀시에트에서 누쿠스까지, 타슈겐트에서 서울까지
아! 끝없는 유랑길 가로등을 꺼라
무엇이 이토록 조국을 낯설게 하는가
이 목숨 다 바쳐서 조국광복 찾는다면 한이 없소
불꽃 같은 생애 총구의 이슬로 사라져 갔고
종횡무진 연해주를 누비며 적을 잡던 무적의 호랑이
봄 잔디밭 위에 끊임없이 한얼의 꽃을 피운 시선
산 너머 그곳에는 고향 있건만
죽어도 나의 소원은 조국의 해방일세
사월의 노래는 지축에 사무쳐
한 잔 들고 한 잔 부어 첫닭이 울도록
밤새도록 퍼올린 브라지미르 안은
화폭마다 옮겨져 주인을 반기누나
우즈베크 번영과 영광의 기치를 들고…….

Master Poet(Ahn Brazimir)

Ma---
You keep anxious with the childlike face;
What are you guilty of?
With his continuous brush stroke
Ahn Brazimir is pulling out his grief
Buried deep in his heart.
What drove us out to the barren salt land?
Honggyungrae Disturbance, Korea-Russia Treaty, Russia-Japan War
As well as the Japanese Annexation of Korea, Bolsheviki Revolution,
And March 1st Independence Movement....
Furthermore, some corrupt officials who pray for more blessing in a river
After they stored hypocrisy and authority in a Grand Icebox.
While the darkness can only afford to misery
Ah, turn the street lamps off in the endless wandering way
Which runs from Tashkent to Seoul.
What made his country so strange to him?
There was no other wish to him
But to get the independence of his country.
His fiery life was gone by their rifles;
He was like a tiger unrivaled in the Maritime Provinces of Siberia.
He was also a master poet
Who caused the continuous blooming of poetry.
His only wish was the independence of his country
Though he could return to his home just beyond a mountain.
An April song was diffused all over the world;
Brazimir Ahn is pulling out his grief all through the night
And he is flying over the sky as a master poet,
With the flag of glorious and prosperous Uzvecstan.

미녀와 트로이 목마

운 좋게 요 며칠 동안
우리는 열 일곱 잔의 와인을 마시며
십 년 원한 품에 애달픈 정조를 노래한다
먼 옛날 계수나무 아로새긴 할렌의 알몸은
하얀 밤 조각달로 흘러만 가는데
못 오는 왕비 몸이면 왕 한 목숨 보낼 것을
어쩌다 십 년 하루 잊으랴
에게해 파도 깊이 스며드는 스파르타 메넬라우스여
나는 살구꽃 올리브 그늘에서 보리수를 그리며
아나톨리아 신화에 누워 행과 연을 갈아 엎다
거기 트로이 왕자 파리스 탐욕은 하늘을 찔러
메넬라우스 왕의 옹달샘을 훔친 치마 속 아야기를
트로이 목마는 수 천년 계속하고 있었다
목화꽃 아름답게 피었다 지고 피고
검고 검은 흑해수는 보스볼라스 말마라해를 지나
에게, 지중해로 새로워져 왔는데
트로이 목마는 파리스왕을 죽이고 트로이를 지켜 왔다
그리고 세세년년 왕비의 휘파람은 목화솜 불지르다
차나칼레 트루왕궁이여 불타는 파리스를 지켜 보았는가
신화와 통정하며 트로아 전쟁을 갈무리하는 그대여
너는 아느냐 이 폐허에 머리 조아리는 비련의 시인을
트로이 목마는 아테네의 신전 앞에 섰고
가련한 시인은 그 앞에 서서 기도를 한다
그리스 용사들은 불을 뿜어 문 열린 트로이는 사라져 갔다
미치도록 섹시한 활활 타오르고

헬렌의 치마 속 탐닉은 지금도 허공에 날고 있다
위선은 죽어 폐허만 남기고 정의는 죽어 목화로 피었구나
영웅은 죽어도 역사는 남는 것 트로이 목마는 오늘도
차나칼레 트루바를 지키고 서서 헬렌을 증언한다

Beauty and the Trojan Horse

For a few days I was lucky
To drink seventeen glasses of wine,
Singing a song of a faithful lady
Who was constant for ten years.
Once upon a time Henlen's naked body
Carved on the laurel tree
Is flowing over the white moon.
She could not have forgotten those days
She spent without her husband.
Oh, Spartan Menelaus!
You haunt on those waves of the Aegean Sea.
I am writing a poem on the Anatolian myth
Under the Olive tree.
The Tojan Horse was telling a story
On the Trojan prince Paris
Whose stole the love of Menelaus's wife.
Flowers of cotton bloom and fade away
Thou managed the Trojan War
With an unrivaled insight of the myth.
Art thou aware of this sorrowful poet
Who gives a deep bow in this ruins?
The Trojan Horse stood
In front of the Athenian sanctuary;
A poor poet is praying at the very place.
The Greek warriors poured out fires

Destroying the Troy.
Now a sexual myth is glowing to madness;
Another greed for Helen is flying across the sky.
A hypocrisy is dead to leave the ruins;
Justice is dead to bloom into cotton flowers.
A hero is alive in the history;
The Trojan Horse testifies Helen's story.

루마니아의 마지막 밤

평온의 짙은 어둠을 가르고
기다리는 불빛이 조금씩 새기 시작했다
물안개 때문이었을까
마음을 간섭하는 외로등 하나 안 보이다가
뜻밖에 LG가로등이 병렬로 환영한다
차창 밖 물방울에 얼굴을 가리는 부크레스트
동유럽 평원에 한 도시는
그렇게 쉬 몸풀지 않고
길손의 눈을 흐리고 있었다
어둠과 뒤섞여 내리는 진눈깨비
그 속을 헤매는 광고등의 빛살 중에 '대우모터'
거리를 질주하는 낯익은 자동차에 몸을 실려
루마니아 대륙을 누비고 있다
무엇이 그토록 지난 이야기를 하게 하는가
이방에서 은신중인 한 사업가의 진실을
누더기 호텔 침대 밑에 숨기고 나는
네스날 오펫드 국제공항으로 달리는 차창에서
새벽을 가르며 다시 만났다
난수표 그대로

The Last Night in Rumania

A waiting streak of light was streaming
Trough the calm darkness.
Was it due to the wet fog?
No street light was seen to interrupt my mind;
Suddenly LG ad lights welcome a traveler.
Raindrops on the car window was screening Bucharest.
Without any interest of showing up,
A city in the huge planes of East Europe
Was blurring the eyesight of a traveler.
It snowed mixed with rain in darkness;
Among lots of ad lights another familiar ad sign
Came into my eyesight: Daewoo Motors.
In a familiar car a traveler is carried
Here and there in the Rumanian field.
What made some old stories flash through his mind?
A businessman hid his truth under the hotel bed,
Leaving for International Airport;
At dawn he met with the truth again
Without solving a table of random numbers.

무심

나는 따뜻한 체온을 느끼며
미증유의 그녀 숨소리를 헤아린다
얼마나 깊은 곳에서 꿈은
잉태하고 있을까
늘어지는 허리에서 자꾸만
함몰하는 숨의 깊이를 몰라 헤맨다
23시 59분 2002. 10. 27
1분의 초심이 25시로 내달리는 무심
나는 순환의 이치를 터득한다
생명이 있는 존재로서

Indifference

Appreciating the warm heat of a woman
I am counting the numbers of her breathing.
Can a dream be conceived in such a depth?
I am at a loss not knowing the depth of her gasping
Which comes from her waist.
Now it's one second to 24 on October 27th in 2002.
One more second may drive me
Into the state of indifference of 25 o' clock.
I realize the truth of circulation
As an living existence in the world.

드라큐라 성

시인은 죽고 없어도
시는 범람하는 세상
시의 품속에서 하품이라도 할라치면
위대한 시인으로 뜻 받쳐 들고
돈 떨어지면 쓰레기가 된다

정신은 죽고 없어도
육체는 환락가에 범람하는 세상
몸뚱아리 사치에 묻은 것 탕진하면
병들은 영육이 널브러져
악마를 살찌운다
내 스스로 시인이라 말하기 전에

오늘은 시험대에 서보련다
아직도 자연이 살아 숨쉬는
사랑의 미로 드라큐라 성

Dracula Castle

While poets are all dead to exist any more,
Poems are overflowing in the world;
If a poet scribbles in the bosom of poetry,
He is esteemed to be a great poet.
However, he is thrown as a garbage
If he runs short of money.

While the spirit is dead to exist nay more,
Bodies are overflowing in the world.
If all the lavish ornaments over the bodies are gone,
Sick bodies are left to feed the evil;
Even before I call myself a poet.

Today I will step on the scaffold.
Dracula Castle stands still
Like a labyrinth of love,
Where Nature is still alive.

겨울 달

때론 유혹 받고 싶은
호올로 긴 겨울 밤의 달
끝내 자살을 불러오는 운률
황홀한 애상이여.

그 속에 전설을 듣던 노인은
낭떠러지 창 밖으로 걸어 나가고
달빛 가락에 취한 처녀는
그를 보며 동맥을 끊는다.

매혹적인 사람과
그를 사랑하는 모든 생명들은
사루비아 꽃잎 같은 선혈에
뒤엉켜 거짓을 줍는다.

The Moon of Winter

Sometimes, the moon in the long wintry
night likes to fall itself in attraction.
A rhythm capable of invoking suicide a
charming sorrow.

An old man listening to the legend walk
toward a precipice.
And while seeing him, a maiden
intoxicated with the moonlight cuts her
artery.

An attractive man and everything loving
him pick up lies in blood as like red
flowers.

커피향 예찬

꽃내음 풀내음도 아닌 길
온 세상이 초록의 연분에 끈끈하다.
꽃향기 풀향기 뿌리 열매 향기가
동서남북 사람 사는 곳마다
마약처럼 파고들어
그윽한 시향 실어 날으매
이 얼마나 가슴 벅찬 놀람이냐

외로운 고행길에 이정표도
꽃도 아니오 풀도 아니오.
사막을 누비는 선인장의 찜
이 한 잔의 검붉은 아편향
한 번 맛보고 다시 또 다시
한 맛에 한량없는 즐거움
구수한 향기가 털구멍에 머문다.

The Cult of Coffee

On a road not scented with flower, or herbage
The world is sticky with the green fate.
The odor of flowerage, the odor of
herbage, the odor of roots spread out all
over the world like drugs.
A sweet scent of poetry floats in the sky.
My heart is too full for wonder.

There is no milepost, flower, or herbage
on a lonely road.
A cactus swaggering about a desert
A cup of black scent of opium
Taste, and taste again, and again
Endless joy
Good scent stay in the hole of feather.

레몬 예찬

빛깔도 정갈한 품위
신선한 맛깔이 묻어나는 살결을
젖가슴 짜듯 애무하면
처녀 젖이 주루루 흐른다.
코 끝을 찌르는 독한 향기가
생살 비린내를 삼키며
입안 가득 주정을 녹여
어디론지 까마득히 멀어져 가는
나의 욕심 그 뒤에 따라오는 진붉은
흑장미가 피어난다.

The Cult of Lemon

A figure in possession of clean lights
If one fondles skins in possession of
sweet and pure scent,
A maiden' s milk flows down.
A poisonous scent swallows in a fishy smell.
And melt down alcohol filled with a mouth.
My advice keeps going away at a great distance.
A dark and red rose following it comes into bloom.

아! 오!
― 근하신년

아! 한 해가 진다
해와 달은 변함없는 교감으로
쉼없이 속삭이는데
한강, 다뉴브강, 에게해, 태평양
물결 청청 푸르소서
오! 새해가 온다
평화의 나래 아름다운 추억이
살구(야생) 꽃처럼 피는데
사랑이 푸른 하늘만큼
당신과 내가 하나 되소서

Ah, Oh!
— Happy New Year

Oh! This year has come to a close.
The sun and the moon whisper to each
other ceasellessly
With mutual responses.
The Han River, the Danube River, the
Aegean Sea, and the Pacific Ocean,
I wish them to be more bluish.
Oh! New Year has come to a open.
The beautiful memories on the Wing
of peace burst into bloom
Like apricot blossoms.
In blue sky full of love.
I wish you and I be one.

달 예찬

초저녁 달은 고향이 그립고,
새벽 달은 어머니가 보고 싶다.
저녁 달은 친구가 그립고,
센 새벽 달은 연인이 보고 싶다.
눈썹 달은 무서움이 생기게 하고
중천만원은 사색에 빠지게 한다.

저녁 하늘 가득 채운 달 정답게 훈훈하고
새벽 하늘 가득 채운 달 이성인양
차갑다
모닥불처럼 차가운 달을 보노라면
계수나무 금도끼가 확연하여
눈으로 볼 수 없는 인생길이 보인다.

달아 달아 밝은 달아
푸른 시절 놀던 달아
구름 속에 숨바꼭질
천진무구 장난끼가
깨우치며 찾아가는
사람 사는 이성일세.

The Cult of the Moon

The moon in the early evening longs for home.
The moon at dawn longs for mother.
The moon in the evening longs for a friend.
The strong moon at dawn longs for a lover.
The eyebrow-shaped moon arouse fear.
The full moon pluck up thoughts.

The moon filled with the sky in the
evening becomes warm.
The moon filled with the sky at dawn
becomes cold as like a campfire.
We can find a gold ax in the moon.
We can see our invisible life.

Oh, the moon, moon, bright moon
Amusing moon in blue ages
Playing hide-and-seek in the clouds
arouses simple and pure pleasantry.
It is the reason of human beings.

살구나무와 보리수는 너무나 닮아 있다

저자는 어떠한 소재로 창작을 할지라도 그 작품 속 그의 인격
이 배여 있고 기품이 반영된다.

1. 창작이란 무엇인가?

2. 시, 소설이란 무엇인가?

3. 왜 쓰는가?

4. 무엇을 쓸 것인가?

5. 어떻게 쓸 것인가?

창작이란 사람의 혼신이라 그 혼신의 소리여야만 독자에게
깊은 감명을 주어 상상의 나래가 가능하다. 이것이 『고려달
빛』의 표상이자 이념이다.

Wild apricot looks like Borisu

It is reflected the personality and thoughts of a writer in his works no matter which materials.

1. What is the writing poetry, novels?

2. What is the poetry and novels?

3. What makes you to write?

4. What do you write about?

5. How do you write?

Writing is the soul of a writer. Also the readings are expressed deeply by the only voice of soul and they give a full play of their imagination. That is the idea of 『The Moon Light of Corea』.

동방 달빛

달아 달아 밝은 달아
우리님 노는 달아
그기 그기 계수나무 꿈나무
세세년년 황금이요
영겁에 우리 사랑 희망이다

이글이글 불꽃 안아
이다지도 냉철한가
여기여기 살구나무 꿈나무
산토끼도 집토끼도
떡방아 쿵덕쿵덕 노래한다

사랑 사랑 내 사랑아
동방에 높이 뜬다
잠시 행복 이를 수가 어쩌면
너와 나는 우리 모두
영원한 한 짝 오직 한 길 돈다.

The Moon Light of Corea

Dara Dara the bright moon
She is playing in the moon
There are, there are the dreaming tree of great Gesu tree
World and world, year and year it is gold
It is everlasting hope

Egl Egl holding the flame in the mind
for goodness sake it is cool heart
here and here are dream tree, wild apricot
a wild rabbit and domesticated rabbit in the moon
they sing sing qundak qundak like a flour mill

Dorling Loving oh my love
It rises high at the east sky
Hippy's happiness for goodness sake
You and I, everybody
Forever, we turn all along in the one way

동방의 빛

새하얀 어둠에서
영그는 고려달빛
오 동방의 보리수 꽃잎 열고
"시심을 통한 세계 형제애"
평화를 사랑으로 추구하는
우주묵객을 초빙합니다.

한 바람은 한바탕
부패한 넘침의 충돌
그 문명의 장막을 밀어내고
여명의 깃발 높이 흔드는
동방의 새 아침을 주목하시오
자연, 생명, 인간, 문명이
뿌리 정맥으로 솟아
살구꽃 문화를 보시합니다

한 발 옮기면 수천길 지옥
그 몸부림의 외마디 비명에
뿌리채 말라가는
지양의 거름을 주십시다
무소불위 탐닉으로 채워가는
변절의 호사한 꽃꿈 잡으러
짙푸른 이슬에 무지개 찾는
시혼 불태우며……

신비하고 오묘한 자연질서
오! 저 장엄하게 솟는 불덩이
가슴으로 끓어 안는
화합의 극치를
새김질 토설하는
동방의 달빛 그 높고 아름다움……

새하얀 어둠에서
영그는 고려달빛
오 동방의 보리수 꽃잎 열고
"시심을 통한 세계 형제애"
평화를 사랑으로 추구하는
우주묵객을 초빙합니다.

The Light of Corea

In the dazzling darkness
the light of Corea becomes mature
Oh! the petal of Bobhendrum in Corea opens
World brotherhood and peace through poetry
Pursuing the peace and love
I invite you

One wind,
a collision of corrupt flowing
pushing out the curtain of civilization
shaking high the flag of dawn
attention! the morning of Corea
nature, life, human, culture
is made to vein rising
Let's see the culture of apricot

A walk, the hell
a scream of struggling
becomes dry absolutely
let's fertilize
filled with greed
chasing the void dream of treachery
don't lose the blue sky
pursuing the rainbow and dew
devote yourselves of the poetry

The cycle of nature
Oh! the rising flame solemnly
hugging with heart
ruminating
the light of Corea, the beauty ······

In the dazzling darkness
the light of Corea becomes mature
Oh! the petal of Bodhendrum in Corea opens
World brotherhood and peace through poetry
Pursuing the peace and love
I invite you

이상은 차다

봄바람 이는 바람 언덕에
기러기 날개 푸르른 하늘
오시는 손님 반갑고요
가시는 손님 정겨웁게
새 희망 굴렁쇠 깃발 달고
세상 문 활짝 펴 우정 심어
시선이 꽃펴야 평화가 온다
동방에 높이 뜬 달빛은 차다
되돌아 되돌아 원류를 찾아
토종꽃 심어서 진리 깨닫고
바른 말 외쳐서 순리를 키워
제비 오는 토양 보람 넘친다.

An Ideal is Cool

In the hill where spring winds blow
The wings of a wild goose, blue sky
Welcome the coming guest,
Farewell, the departing guest
The flag with new hope
Open the world gate and plant friendship
Blossom the poem to be peaceful
The moon in the east is cool
Return return to the origin
Plant the original flower and realize the truth
Shout the right opinion and grow the fact
In the soil where a swallow flying it is worthy

등대지기의 노래

세상 말하는 사람 오라
아리 아리 아리랑 알리오
그것은 자연의 이치 공상소설
모든 빛은 거룩한 밤에 있다.

세상 고려 달빛 비쳐라
아리 아리 아리랑 알리오
온화한 어린이 평온의 잠
모든 빛은 거룩한 밤에 있다

세상 하늘 평화 오라
아리 아리 아리랑 알리오
그것은 우리 새 고향 최고 희망
모든 빛은 거룩한 밤에 있다.

The Song of a Light House Keeper

Come, people to say about the world
Ahri Ahri Ahrirang Alrio
That is the science fiction, the reason of nature
All light is in the holy night

Bright, the moon light of Corea in the world
Ahri Ahri Ahrirang Alrio
A mild infant slept silently
All light is in the night

Come, the peace of the world in the sky
Ahri Ahri Ahrirang Alrio
That is our new hometown, the best hope
All night is in the night.

노 시인은 죽지 않는다
— 오직 고려 달빛처럼 영원할 뿐이다

노 시인은 죽지 않는다.
오직 고려 달빛처럼
영원할 뿐이다.

비록 매일 밤마다
달은 볼 수 없지만
어디쯤 우릴 지켜보고 있다

세상 사람들아 말하라
길을 밝히는 등대가
왜 생겼는지를

Old Poets Never Die
— They Only Eternalize As Eternal as "The Moon Light of Corea"

Old poets never die.
They only eternalize as eternal as
The Moon Light of Corea

Even light never been looked
One night after night
The moon kept us at anywhere

Let' s say people in the world
Why, it has been light that
A lighthouse keeper informed life

등대지기의 노래 2

사랑하고 있다고 말하라
사랑하고 있다고 말하라
칠흑의 적막을 깨어
울리는 소리 새 소리
여명을 몰고 오는 그대
그대 당신의 박동에
한숨을 토한다

양심의 어둠에
세상을 망치고
가정도 부서지고
스스로 상심하는 여울목이
맴도는 육신

사랑하고 있다고 말하라
사랑하고 있다고 말하라
밤새워 숨어 본
태양을 마시며 요동하는
은빛 파도를 탄다
그를 위해 시를 짓는
등대지기 노래

The Song of a Lighthouse Keeper 2

Let's say love it
Let's say love it
Breaking the darkness of death
rising his voice with mutual voice
only one that come on with the tender light
Because your heart voice
deeply breathe out

Because thought in living in the darkness
That destroy the world on
and somehow family is breaking
with self body of lost world
It's in neck river that don't water mill

Let's say love it
Let's say love it
seeing keeper all night
playing when he drinks the sun
mixing in silvery waves
Writing poems for him
The song of a lighthouse keeper

등대지기의 노래 3

당신을 사랑하오
당신을 사랑해요
밤마다 밤새워 당신을 사랑합니다
밤은 나의 삶이요 당신의 인생
저 바다와 더불어 멀리 내 사랑 지킨다

저 등대의 불빛은
그 스스로를 위해 밝히고 있지 않지만
자신의 열정이 불타기에
저 풍랑 어두움의 길을 연다

당신을 사랑하오
당신을 사랑해요
밤마다 밤새워 당신을 사랑합니다
밝은 태양이 당신을 불태워 버릴지라도
아름다운 밤은 당신 인생을 기다린다

The Song of a Lighthouse Keeper 3

I love you
I love your it
I love you all night all
That night is my to live too you
Love me and keep me away with sea

A light in a lighthouse
But don't shine for himself
because his passion in burning
Open my way on there dark heavy seas

I love you
I love your it
I love you all night all
even though fair sun burned down you
Beautiful night wait for your life

등대지기의 노래 4

죽엄의 그림자는
칠흑같이 빛이 나고
떠나가는 무수한 별들
반딧불처럼 사라져 간다
으흠! 영원한 생명
햇빛이 공간에 차면
홀로 사랑 노래 부른다

짙누른 먹구름이
힘겨움에 밀려가며
솟구치던 빗줄기도
촉촉히 가슴 젖는 가랑비 된다
으흠! 영원한 삶
하늘이 무너져도
솟아날 구멍은 있다

짙푸른 물감으로
덧칠하는 비인 마음
수수만년 제 몸살은 빛
영원으로 이어질 수가
으흠! 영원한 사랑
순간에 생겨나 지고마는
삶의 참뜻 깨우친다

The Song of a Lighthouse Keeper 4

The shadow of the die
glitter all the same paint dark color
To leave low many stars
die away just the same the glow a firefly
Ehm! eternal for life
When sunshine over pour in the air
only one sing a love song

That have pressed the black cloud
it be pressed out by don't measure strength
That leap up a stem rain
when come by it is drizzling
Ehm! eternal living
Even though heaven fall on earth
Where is hole of to jump strength

On soulful mind paint to paint
with color of happy greenees
It is light of self to die eternally
Who is who everlasting
Ehm! eternal daring
A momentour birth never eternally live
anybody regain one's spirit of life

등대지기의 노래 5

누구는 언제나 스스로를 태워 버린다

태양은 너무 외롭다
태양은 너무 따뜻하다
태양은 너무 냉철하다
태양은 너무 정이 많다
태양은 너무 매정하다
태양은 너무 가깝다

당신 따르는 것들 너무 많지만
당신은 언제까지 혼자일 뿐
당신 가슴은 수천도 용광로
당신 스스로를 태우고 또 태운다
당신 뜨거운 가슴 때문에
당신 외면한 세상은 꽁꽁 언다

그대는 나쁜 날 없고
그대는 우울한 삶 없다
그대는 좋아하지 않지만
그대는 미워하지 않는다
그대는 그 자리에서
그대는 안 죽는다

까닭에 그 빛은 위대한 영원이다

The Song of a Lighthouse Keeper 5

Who's lighting anytime that be in flame

The sun is to feel lonely over oneself
The sun is too warm to oneself
The sun is cooling over oneself
The sun is over feeling all along world
The sun is never feeling oneself
The sun is nearly only one in the universe

What is many that like you
But you are only one forever
Your heart is burning to smell high
Yourself are burning too burning
Because of your heart is burning
The world is cooling without your love

Thou never look upset one day
Thou never had any bad in the light
Thou never like whoever
Thou never hate whoever
Thou never are wherever only one
Thou never die that be oneself

Because the light is forever with greatness.

등대지기의 노래 6

공간에는 오직 하나의 빛만 있다
이 순간 태양은 가득히 차 오른다
우주에 유일한 빛
그것은 너무너무 멀리 있지만
우리는 오직 하나 자연 질서

친구야 오너라 친구 친구야
함께 손잡고 노래 부르자
꽃 피고 새 우는 낙원을 찾아서
영겁의 길 홀연히 나선다

진달래, 복숭아, 살구꽃, 옹달샘
중장비로 부숴 버린 자리에
청청 솔림 파 옮겨 놓고
요절을 재촉하는 악마의 곡예
언 가슴 쓸어안고 열반에 들면
청푸른 하늘 내려앉아 연화 핀다.

The Song of a Lighthouse Keeper 6

There is only light on the space
Now, sun when it is sunning
more and more
There is only light on the universe
That is how many miles away from here
However, we are among only one

Let᾽ s come, trends with trends, too
Let᾽ s sing hands in hands, too
We are hoping paradise to sing birds
and flower
Naturally start, forever walking way

The an azalea, a peach, an apricot blossoms
and spring water,
where are broken by big machine
Let᾽ s move about to greenwood pines
Let᾽ s pass early to die fancy of evil fiends.
If there are into Nirvana at farm cool heat,
A lotus flower where green sky down,

자연 현대 노래

만약에 당신의 심장이 건강하길 원한다면
인류평화를 위한 일을 하시오
만약에 당신이 좋은 행복을 찾고 있다면
진정한 문화를 승화하는 문명 사이에서
문제의 대화를 찾으시오.
정신문화를 위해 나서지 않겠습니까.
세계시인대회 세계시인대회
그 모든 것 사랑 속에 있고
그 모든 것 우리와 함께 이루려니
그 곳을 위해 점점 나아갈 때
푸른 하늘은 우리들 머리 위에 있습니다.

오직 지구는 하나, 인류는 하나

Song of W. C. P.(Natural Modernism)

If you want to your healthy heart
Let' s working ministry for peace
If you want to good happy
Conversation with dialogue is
Between civilization for spirit culture
Are we meeting for that
World Congress of Poets W. C. P.
Love is knowing all that
We may be together that
Then we being to make better better
Blue sky is on our head

Only one is the globe and the mankind

왜 당신은

당신은 왜 나를 싫어합니까
나는 당신을 좋아합니다
당신은 누구일까요. 바로 당신이지
그렇게 당신을 미워합니다

당신은 왜 나를 싫어합니까
나는 당신을 좋아합니다
한 떨기 이른 봄날에 민들레 꽃같이
샛노란 정열에 나는 애타요
그렇게 당신을 미워합니다

Why You

Why do you dislike me
I like you
Who are you. It's you
I hate you so

Why do you dislike me
I like you
Like dandelion in the early spring
I'm anxious at yellow passion
I hate you so

강변에 서서

멀리 이국 땅처럼
포플러 솔잎 사이로 등대불 조네
온종일 숨지는 애절함을
붉게 태워 버리려는
지평선에 홍조를 토하고
구름은 퇴색해 버린 자신의 노여움에
무지개 빛으로 울고 있네

바람 안은 돛단배
방향 없이 떠나가는데
모질게도 얼룩진 재색 철교는
강 위에서 졸고 있네
힘차게 내달은 여운은 사라지고
여기 우뚝선 침묵의 가슴에
풍성한 자연의 황홀함이
깊은 감사를 낳는다.

저의 느낌은 그랬습니다.
철로를 달아오르게 내려 쬐던 태양이
쇠진하여 쓰러져 가지만
그 여운은 구름의 빛깔을 바꿔 놓고 있습니다
그와 같이 만물의 이치는 서로 연결되어 돌고 도는
우주의 법칙을 깊이

Standing on the Riverside

Like an alien land,
A beacon lamp was asleep between the polar and pine leaves
Burning sun for the all day long
Vomit red light on the horizon
To burn out sadness of last moment
Clouds are crying as the rainbow color
Because of the their anger which discolored

A sailing ship in the wind
Is leaving without direction
Gray street bridge stained ruthlessly
Is asleep on the river
Strong feeling disappeared
Here heart of the standing silence
Fruitful ecstasy of nature
Make deep gratitude

I felt like that
Even sun that make steelrail road hot so fall
That feeling changed the color of clouds
Like this natural law goes round connected each other
The law of universe deeply

윤에게

길손의 애환은 가슴 속에 여미고
스쳐 가는 초목은 옛 정을 그립게 한다.
이별만은 슬프더라 이별만은 야속터라.
속리고속 스피커의 유행가 가락에도
시름시름 젖어드는 차창가 나그네
소망같이 괴로운 것이 어디 있으랴
소망같이 외로운 것이 어디 있으랴
흘러간 길손 너의 추억 알고파라
황홀한 석양은 지고 대지에는
장막이 내리고 너도 가고 나도 가야지

인정은 멀어지고 세상은 삭막해지고
양심은 육체의 노예가 되고
황금의 횡포는 날로 심해지고
그래서 우리는 서로를 속이고
그러나 고독한 그 심정은 진실이외다.
우리는 깊은 대화가 있었지
우리는 서로를 알고 있었지
우리는 서로를 용서하고 있었지

To Yoon

Sadness of wonderer bear in my mind
Grazing grass and trees make me miss olden love
Only parting is sad, only parting is inhospitable
Wanderer in the window side feel sad by the popular
song through the speaker in the Sokri Express
How can it exist suffering thing like wishes
How can it exist lonely thing like wishes
I' d like to know you wander' s past memory
The wonderful declining sun set, on the earth
Silence maintain, you leave and I' ll leave too

Human kindness grow distant and human world is dreary
Conscience became a slave of body
And arrogance of gold become serious day by day
So we deceive each other
But lonely heart is the truth
We had serious conversation
We knew each other
We forgave each other

내장산

붉게 타는 단풍
탐스럽게 익은 감
자연의 조화는 찬연히 빛난다.
인적은 차츰 끊기고
내장산 계곡엔
단풍과 바위 숨어드는 냇물과 그리고 나,
대지 위에는 차츰 어려움이 짙어 오고
석양에 마지막 정열을 불태우던 잎새도
이제 빛을 잃으니
미움도 사랑도
슬픔도 기쁨도
욕망도 갈등도
쉬어 가는 나그네의 추억이려니
칠흑 같은 어두움과 적막이
이제 나도 저 불빛을 찾아가야지

Naejang Mt.

Burning maple in red
Ripe persimmons appetizingly
Harmony of nature shine brilliantly
Human traces is disappeared gradually
In the valley in Naejang Mt.
Stream hiding maples and rocks and me
On the earth, difficulty become thick gradually
And burning leaves last passion in the sunset
Now lost their lights
Hates and loves,
Sorrow and joy,
Desire and discord,
May be the memory of wonderer in relax
Dead darkness and silence
Now I will go to find that light

미소

꽃향기 머금은
봄이 오는 길목에

수줍은 미소짓는
노란 싹이 아까워

한 발짝 비켜 서면
내딛는 발 밑에

해묵은 낙엽의
애달픈 비명소리

그대로 지나치긴
너무나 가엾어

상처난 그 잎 주워
고웁게 펴들고

겨우내 못 다한
사연을 나누며

봄아씨 오시는 길
낙엽 함께 걷는다.

Smile

Entertaining flower fragrance
On the way of coming spring

Shy smile
Yellow bud is regrettable

So I move a step
Unter the foot

Sad scream sound
Old fallen leaves

So pity
I pass by like that

I pick wounded leaves up
And unfold prettily

Share a story
Which hadn' t for the winter

I' m walking with fallen leaves
On the road where spring lady is coming

고향

긴 세월! 옛 고향 돌아오니
산천은 변함없건만 어쩐지 타향같으다
형제들이 심은 나무는 자라
빨갛게 열매를 주렁 달아
가슴에 밀쳐 오는 세월의 무상함이여
감회에 넘쳐 소리치고 싶지만
옛 벗은 멀리에 뿔뿔이 헤어지고
낯선 얼굴, 보는 얼굴이 예가 아니로구나

아버님 소자가 왔습니다
고이 잠드신 산천이여
오랜 세월 찾아오지 못하였습니다
가슴을 조이며 생각에 생각을
고사리손 힘들여 심은 언덕 위 밤나무
나름대로 알알이 밤이 달렸구나
오솔길 정자나무 옛 그대로인데
어쩌면 사람은 옛사람이 아니로구나

Hometown

Long time! Since I return to my old hometown
Mountain and streams had not been changed but
seems to me strange land
Trees my brothers plant grow
So have many fruits
The frailty of time in my heart
I'd like to shout by the deep impression
But my old friends scattered in all directions
Strange faces, what I see the face is different from the
old times

Father, I came here
Sleeping silently mountains and streams
I had not been for a long time
I'm fidgety and think
Chestnut trees on the hill planted hardly by children
Have chestnuts
A big tree in the narrow path is same as the past
But people are not same as the past

생각

태산 위에
푸른 하늘이
모두의 가슴 속에
사랑이 있다네
별처럼 빛나는
세계 평화
오라
영원히 오라

Thinking

There is the blue sky
On the mountain
There is a love
In everybody' s chest
Twinkle like stars
World peace
Welcome
Welcome to see again

패싸움

노-오란 강아지 한 마리가 개뼉다귀를 물고 어슬렁 어슬렁거
리는데 까아만 개새끼 한 마리가 다가서며 그것을 빼앗으려
덤빈다. 노-오란 강아지 짖어대는 찰나 개뼉다귀 떨어지고 까
아만 강아지 비명 소리에 까아만 어미 뒤엉키어 아수라
장……
골목길은 차단되고 흥분한 개새끼 싸우는 소리가 왁자지 껄
고요한 아침 정적을 깨트리는데 배기 가스의 아지랑이 무늬
로 그 일은 피어 오르고 라이터에 양담배 피워 문 보신병들은
기름진 살찐 놈의 고랑에 걸려 들어 세단차 트렁크에서 숨 못
쉬는데 고놈의 개뼉다귀 귀신은 이 아침에도 영락없이 발길
에 걸린다

A Gang Fight

When a yellow puppy walks around with a dog bone, black dog is approaching to take it. As soon as yellow puppy bark, dog bone is dropped. As soon as black dog take it, mother dog rush to them by the barking sound of yellow dog and by the screaming of the black dog, it's mother fight with them so the place become mass······

A side street closed and fighting sound of exited dog break the silence of morning so this happened to have shape of wasted gas and army for self protection who is smoke western cigarette by lighter is caught by fat person so can't breath in the sedan car. But the ghost of dog bone entangled in my feet this morning without any slip.

신세대 바람아

바람아
너는 어디에서 와서
어디로 가는 걸까
목선 하나 없는 막막 바다
누군가를 사랑하고픈
텅 빈 가슴 언저리에
무심한 파도가 철썩이는구나

바람아
너는 어이어이하여
너는 마음대로 가는 걸까
폐허 농가 옥답마다
지쳐진 곰팡이 언저리
곰삭는 대들보 내 맘 같구나

Wind of New Age

Wind
Where are you from
Son where are you going
No wooden boat in the wide sea
I' d like to love somebody
On the edge of my early heart
Only heedlessness waves keep lapping

Wind
Why
Why are you going your own convenience
Every ruin, farmhouse, fertile paddy-field
Edge of tired mold
Wearing off girder, it seems to be my heart

화련

넓고 넓은 대륙에서
대양을 건너는 징검다리를
이름하여 화련, 빛 부신 요정
천지조화의 무진한 걸작은
생명의 근원을 심오하게도
구곡동 절벽에 게시하고 있다.

잔은 돌려도 병은 돌리지 마오
병은 돌려도 잔은 돌리지 말지어다
처음 짜릿한 기분 지나 보면 별 것 아닌 것
전부를 돌리면 어지러우니
고개만 성심껏 돌리려므나

진솔한 사랑은 몰라보면서
어쩌다 여자만 알아보는가
밤새도록 뻗쳐 선 미련한 장승아
내가 미워 취하는 건
술뿐만 아니로세

Hwaryun

In the wide continent
Steeping stones walking oceans
We call it Hwaryun, bright Sprite
Great masterpiece of heaven and earth harmony
Notice origin of life in Gugokdong valley

Please pass the glass but don' t pass the bottle
Please pass the bottle but don' t pass the glass
The first impression is not important by time goes by
I feel dizzy when pass all
Please pass only the head sincerely

Son don' t recognize the true person
How do you know only women
Clumsy totem pole standing all night long
Which I' m drunken is not only alcohols.

한양 1394 서울 1994
— 천도 600년 기념에

날마다 해 뜨는 곳
배달의 혈맥은
겨레의 심장에서 숨쉬고
우린 우리들의 태반
장미빛 피로 낙원을 가꾼다

1394 한양 1994 서울은
백운의 기가 삼각에 솟아
좌청룡 우백호가 북악에 머물고
좌수에 낙산응봉 우수엔 인왕이 다가서서
안산을 휘돌아
청계수 명당에 이르러
태조 3년 황포자락 여미며 하늘을 바라보았다

남향 천리 바쁜 걸음 멈추어
흐르는 한수에 염원을 띄우고
바람결에 구름가듯
출렁이는 강물 지나온 길목마다
무궁화가 피고 지고

진정 이제는
수난의 그날들을 귀감으로 다져서
건강한 자연 속에 깨끗한 민족얼을
나눔과 배풂으로 여유로움 길러내어
축복의 하늘과 땅

후손에게 돌려주자

잊혀진 노래 옛 놀던 정
영명하게 되살리고
방화의 슬픔일랑
혼돈의 미움일랑
알 수 있는 구름 속에 실어보내고
은하수 달 가듯
계수나무 노저어라

새 사람 깃을 달고
맑은 영원 속으로
소리없는 장단에 횃불을 밝혀 들고
영욕의 육백년 영을 넘어
소망스런 새 아침
우린 바로 그날 10월 28일
여명을 맞는다

자자손손 이어가고
궁성 용마루에 이끼도 차다
그대여, 오늘의 모습도
민족의 연줄로 묶어진 가지마다
꽃구름 아름답게 기슭에 내리고
자유분방한 신사
깃발도 휘날려

길섶마다 높이 자란 빌딩 숲 마천루와
사통팔달 거미줄로 철마다 달리니
첨단의 섬광이 가슴 가득 피어나
종횡무진 강산에 어린다

빼어난 금수강산
뚜렷한 사계절에
거대한 피질로 쌓여만
가는 쓰레기의 산과 강
자욱한 매연 속에 쌓여가는 지천은
공존의 의미를 새롭게 일깨워
더불어 살아가는 새로운 탄생
아! 모두는 자연 속에 우리여라

눈부시게 아름답고
향기로운 꽃동산
꽃중의 꽃을 피워
휘영청 뻗은 가지 끝마다
영원과 환기를 잉태게 하며
이 괴로움도 기쁨으로 오리라

삶의 지혜가
옛스런 흰 옷소매에 걸치니
고통에서 얻어지는 명상을
너를 위해 우리들은 마신다.

Hanyang 1394 Seoul 1994
— Transferring Capital 600 years anniversary

The place where the sun rises everyday
The Korean race is breathing
In the heart of the race
We take care of paradise in our placenta
By the rosy blood

In 1394 Hanyang 1994 Seoul
Strength of Baekun goes up Samgak
The blue dragon on the left and white tiger on the
right are staying at Bukak
A mountain and the peak on the left water, on the right
Inwang is approaching closer and whirling Ansan
So they are reaching at good place
Taejo 3 years, I saw the sky with adjusting my
traditional dress

I stopped busy walking
Wafted my wish on flowing water
As the clouds in the wind
Every road flowing in the water
The road of sharon bloom and fall

Now, really
We have to think the past suffering as a model
By sharing and giving
Let' s had over sky and earth of blessing to descendants.

Forgotten song, played affection in the past
perspicaciously recall
sadness of incendiarsm
hate of chaos
Send them back in the clouds as we could know
As the moon in galaxy
Pull on oar at the cinnamon tree

New person sew a collar on a coat
In the clean soul
By the silent rhythm, hold the torchlight
Cross the pass of 600 years glory and shame
New morning of wishes
We meet morning
That day Oct., 28

Children and grandchildren will hand over
Moss in the dragon floor is also cold
You, figure of today
Every branch tied by race's connection
Flower cloud is falling on the edge
Free gentleman
Streaming flag
Building forest at each road and
Running at every season like spider's web
Light of high society is blossom in my heart

So stay in the river

On a wonderful embroidered rivers and mountains
Clear four seasons
But mountains and rivers become trash
Land and sky going had by sooty smoke
Making aware of coexistence meaning newly
New birth living together
Ah, all are people in the nature

Dazzlingly beautiful and
Fragrant flower garden
Bloom flower in the flowers
Every end of big spread branch
Making glory and joy
This suffering will be delight

Wisdom of life
Put on old sleeves
We drink for you meditation
Given by suffering

깊은 가을

산들바람에
푸른 잎새가 울고
갈대가 춤을 춘다

바스락 소리
귀 기울여 손님인가
맨홀에 뒹구는 낙엽의 흐느낌

귀뚜라미 소리
깊어 가는 가을 이야기가
지칠 줄 모르는 자동차 소리에

바람이 분다
잎새를 흔든다
그래도 낙엽은 흐른다

Far Advanced Autumn

By the cool breeze
Blue leaves are crying
Reeds are dancing

Rustling sound
Listening carefully, is the guest out
Sobbing of the leaves rolling over the manhole

Sounds of crickets
Far advanced autumn story
By the continuous sound of automobiles

The wind is blowing
Shaking leaves
Although fallen leaves are flowing

바이칼 호

갈대도 잠들은
고요한 밤에 우는
출렁출렁 물소리만
적막을 깬다

별빛은 서러워
쏟아져 내리고
달빛은 너울너울
수천 미터 수심을 재는데
그 누가 불러주나
애송곡이 들린다

해당화 모듬에
잊혀진 내 님은
애수에 저무나
구름도 떠나기 싫어
산허리 잡고 우는구나
화석처럼 굳어 버린
빙하의 심장부에
선혈을 뿌리며
평화를 심던 사람아!

Lake Baikal

Even reed is sleeping
Only sound of waves cry
Break silence
In the silent night

Straight is sad
And poured down
Moonlight is waving
And measuring several thousands depth of water
Who does sing a song?
I can hear my favorite song

By a bunch of sweet briers
Forgotten my lover has disappeared
By the sadness
Clouds also don't want to leave
So they are catching hillside and crying
Being solid like fossil
On the center of glacier
There is a person
Sprinkling blood and implanting peace

매립장

내 마음의 거울은
어디에 빛이길래
노쇠한 석양이 파도를 능간하나

백석 앞바다로
내달리는 쓰레기차
기라성 이루어
상큼한 해풍이
구린내를 묻어온다

Reclamations Land

Mirror of my heart
Where is the light
The old sunset
Chaff with wave

A trash car is going
To the offshore areas of white stone
Making a galaxy
By the fresh sea wind
A foul smell stinks

봉래산 진달래

님은 가 버려도
풀잎은 돋아나네
봉래산 진달래
아름아름 피어나
광음을 못 이겨
연분홍 퇴색한다
사랑은 가 버려도
시절은 남아서
진달래 망울질 때면
또 다시 나 홀로
이 산길 걸어가리.

Azaleas of Bonglae-Mt.

Even though my lover has gone
But leaves of grass are grown
Azaleas of Bonglae-Mt.
Bloom gently
It changed to pink color
By the time and tide
Even though my lover has gone
But time is stayed
So in the azaleas blossom time
I will walk alone again
In this mountain path

향수

나는 네 이름을 쓴다
그 노래 고향의 봄아!
내 삶이 시작된 민들레 언덕에
벌거숭이 고독이 하늘을 보면
먼 산
지리산 양천강은 굽어지고
음 매 메아리친 안산 허리골에
어미소 방울소리 명상 속에 사무쳐 온다
꿈나무 가지가지 그리움 익어간 곳
내 어이 차마

나는 네 이름을 지운다
은밀한 사랑마저 지쳐 쓰러진
쾌락만 무성하게 파헤쳐진 무덤가에
낭비한 젊음의 안가슴처럼
인조된 광채가 눈부신데
홍겹던 콧노래 구성진 이랑에도
악의 꽃 빈 병들이 죽순 같구나
꿈나무 가지가지 그리움 익어간 곳
내 어이 차마

Longing For Home

I'm writing your name
That son, the spring of home!
On the dandelion hill where my life started
When nude solitude looks at the sky
Far mountain
Yangchun river in Jiri mountain is meandering
In the Ansan valley where moo is echoing
Tinkle of cows touch my heart in the meditation
Every branches of dream, the place of longing
How can I do anything!

I'm erasing your name
My secret love become tired and fell down
In a grave where only pleasure is turned up thickly
As youth of wasted mind
Maden light is brilliant
In a patch where people sing a song pleasantly
Devil's flower, empty bottle seem to be bamboo
Every branches of dream tree, the place of longing
How can I do anything!

제대

길고도 먼 삼백리길
숨찬 줄 모르고
단숨에 달려왔외다
그 날에
꽃이 피면 같이 울었고
우수수 낙엽지면
같이 거닐었던 님, 님!
소쩍새 울어줄까 마음 졸이며
노을연 남만 바라보는
오! 그 날은 아름다운 추억 속에
해는 저문다.
거칠은 대지 위에 모래알같이
낙엽 따라 바람 따라
굴러 다녀도
조각달 흐린 빛에
반짝거리고
…에 이은 역사
기둥되려니
온누리 평화 속에
…하시라!

The Cosmic Dual Forces

Long and fair 300ri road
I ran in a breath not knowing I' m out of breath
That day
When the flower blossom, I cried together
When the leaves fall
Lover who walked with me
I' m nervous a cuckoo maybe cry for me
Seeing the sunset through the southern window
Oh! That day is in the beautiful memory
Sur set
Like sand on the rough field
Following fallen leaves, following wind
Even I' m rolling
A crescent is bright by the unclean color
Long history
Being a poll
Please be comfortable
In the peace of the world

외할아버지 산소에서

허무하다 인생의 길
말없는 무덤가에
제 철인 줄만 알고
할미꽃만 피었구나
앞 냇가에 흐르는 물소리는
옛대로
노래하는구나

At the Grave of Grandfather

Vain, the road of life
At the silent grave
A pasqueflower blossom
Even though the season has not coming yet
The water sound on the stream
As the past
Sing a song

먼 훗날

보리밭 고개에 길엔 아카시아숲이 있지요
오월이면 짙은 향내 따라……
오솔길에,
철없는 우리들은 즐거웠습니다.
고사리손 가시내의 긴- 머리는 올라가고,
아카시아 꽃잎 사이
먼 하늘만 바라보노라면
짙은 향 내음은
일어버린 서러움을 달래주었지요.
먼 훗날
남산길 후암동 뒷산에서(서울)
오월이 되면
일어버린 옛날의 그리움에서
혼자만이 해지는 줄 미처 몰랐답니다.
사람들은
부루도자로 아카시아 숲을 파 헤치고
육중한 도서관을 지었답니다.
그 자리에는
긴 머리 가시내도, 짙은 향내도, 파아란 하늘도, 오월도
아무것도 없습니다. 다만 지난 달만이……
지은씨!
모두가 외면해 버린 거기에는 풀과 흙,
아카시아와 파란 하늘이……

그리고 맑은 공기가 있지요.

더려는 모르겠지요. 사람에게 마음준다는 것이, 얼마나
무서운 일인지!
풀 곁에 흙이 있듯이
우리는 남기고 떠날 말을 배웁시다.
지은씨! 속리산이 좋다지요. 아카시아 꽃필 무렵
같이 한 번 가봤으면 합니다. 건강을 빌면서

The Remote Future

In a pass of barley field, there are acacia forest on
the road
On May, following the deep fragrance······
In the narrow path,
We enjoyed thoughtlessly,
Long haired little girl is going up,
Between the leaves of acacia
Seeing the far sky
Deep fragrance
Diverted my mind from the lost sorrow.
The remote future
On Namsan path, in a hill at the back in Hooam dong
On May
By the yearning of lost past
I didn't know the sunset.
People
Digged up acacia forest by the bulldozer
And built great library.
There are no long haired girl, deep fragrance, blue sky,
the May. Only the past is there······
Jieun!
Even people avert their eyes but there are grass and
soil, acacia and blue sky······

And there is fresh air.

Maybe we don't know. How awful thing to give their
mind to someone!
As soil is beside on the grass
Let's learn to say when we leave.
Jieun! People say Sokri Mt. is great about acarcia season.
I'd like to go there with you. I hope you are keeping well.

두만강 처녀

창문을 닫아도
달빛은 숨어들고
마음을 닫아도
사랑은 파고든다

그리움 새순처럼
보헤미안 엘레지
인형 같은 사람들아
두만강 처녀는 어디 갔나

Lady in Duman River

Although I close the window
Moonlight get in by stealth
Although I close my heart
Lover eats into my heart

As a missing shoot
Bohemian elegy
Persons like dolls
Where is a lady in Duman River

들국화 1

시인의 정감으로
꽃잎은 순정을 보듬고
남 모를 골짜기
진혼의 꿈을
만인의 가슴 속에 부른다

순백의 자정으로
파아란 하늘 흰구름에
햇살 타고 내려온
엄마의 미소를
해원으로 실어 보낸다

둥근 달 계수나무
그 옛 이야기
한없이 바라보며
스치는 바람에 별을 헤누나
별을 헤누나

Wild Chrysanthemums 1

By the feeling of the poet
Flower leaves me are holding a pure heart
In the unknown valley
I call the dream of soul
Into the heart of all the people

By the pure and white love
White clouds in the blue sky
Coming down by the sunlight
Let me send mother' s smile
To the sea

Cinnamon tree on the full moon
The old story
Seeing endless
I' m counting stars in the wind
I' m counting stars

그 가을의 찻집

따사로운 해가 기어드는
문틀 잎 새빨간 맨드라미 꿈은
막차를 기다리는
그 가을의 찻집

그녀의 쓸쓸한 얼글에는
정열이 옹이로 굳어 가는
자화상을 그리고 있었다

벌겋게 타는 태양
분수 같은 소나기 가슴
그 빗줄기 사이로
깊어만 가는 우수

그 찻집 맨드라미
진붉은 사연을 지병으로 보듬고
이 가을을 또 보낸다

A Teahouse of Last Autumn

Lightening soft sun
Beside door frame, dream of cockscomb
Waiting the last train
Teahouse of last autumn

On her lonely face,
Passion become hard to node
She was drawn self-portrait

Sun burns red
Heart of shower like fountain
Though that train
Melancholy becomes deeper and deeper

A cockscomb of that teahouse
This autumn goes again with red content of letter with
a chronic disease

개원
— 동국대학 예술대학원 개원에 붙여

그대 알아요
징소리*, 풍경소리*, 가야금소리*
공간의 함성은 지고의 꿈을 향해
지축*의 혈맥으로 영원히 이어갈
예술의 요람 동국이 문을 연다

민들레*보다 끈질기고
장미빛*보다 진붉어라
들국화*보다 향기로운
너의 뜨거운 가슴 너의 차디찬 영혼이
나라 위해 깃발을 든다

그대 알아요
뜨거운 심장이 우주 속에서
푸르디 푸른 하늘*을 열어가며
흰 구름* 노니는 장충단 언덕 위에
예술의 요람* 동국이 문을 연다

아지랑이 나비 춤사위에
종다리* 봄찬가 부르면
어미소* 이랑마다
제비집* 한삼매 또 한삼매
이 모두는 시심이어라

* 징소리-대중의 소리

* 풍경소리-높은 품위의 수신

* 가야금-한민족의 참된 소리

* 지축-세계의 중심

* 민들레-밟혀도 번식하는 생명력

* 장밋빛-열정

* 들국화-우리들의 근본되는 서정

* 하늘-넓고 큰 오직 하나뿐인

* 흰 구름-일하며 배우는 깨끗한 민중

* 요람-베풀며 배우는

* 종다리-수직으로 곧게 처신하며 맑고 고운 소리를 내는 정조

* 어미소-어머니의 태반같이 불변의 소리

* 제비집-장인이 쌓아 올린 업적

* 한삼매-불교에서 말하는 한 가지 일에 집중하는 수행

The Opening of the Academy
— According to the opening of Dongkuk Univ. Art Academy

You know
Sound of gong*, sound of wind bell*, sound of gayakum*
A great outcry of the space is going toward dream
To connect forever by the blood vessel of the earth*
The cradle of art, Dongkuk open the door

More strong and sticky than dandelion*
More red than the rose*
More fragrant than the wild chrysanthemums*
Your hot heart and my cold soul are
Holding a flag for our nation

You know
Hot heart is in the universe
Opening the blue sky*
On the Jangcun hill where white cloud* is wandering
The cradle* of art, Dongkuk open the door

By the dance of butterfly
Skylark's song for the spring
Cow* in every patch
Swallow house*, hansammae* hansammae
This is the mind for the poems

* sound of gong - sound of public

* sound of wind bell - high dignity

* gavagum - true voice of Koreans

* earth - center of the world

* dandelion - strong power of life

* rose - passion

* wild chrysanthemums - our lyricism of origin

* sky - wide and big, only one

* white cloud - working and learning public

* cradle - sharing and learning

* skylark - acting straightly and pretty voice of bird

* cow - unchanged truth like mother's placenta

* swallow house - accomplishment by engineer

* hassammae - concentrating self discipline in Buddhism

입학원서

버스값도 없는 것이 대학을 간다고
오늘은 정월 초이튿날
고려대학 입학원서 마감일이다.
영확이를 찾아가니 미안하고 미안하다.
반찬집 아주머니 초이튿날 무슨 돈을
중앙시장 천막가게 봉연이 문규삼 씨
해동학교 김 선생님께 시험표를 얻고 보니
올빼미 신세가 들어가면 무엇하랴
졸업장을 받아쥐고 명동에서 한 잔 하고
학우들과 무리지어 택시를 잡아타니
인생은 즐겁다고 노래소리 드높구나
에라! 모르겠다
내 팔자가 큰일난다더냐
앞을 보고 못가며는 뒤로 보고라도 가야지
정치대학 합격통지 입학금이 64,200원
어머니가 보내주신 70,000원이 다 나가네
고사리손 두 동생의 피어린 돈일 텐데
나는 잠 못이룬다
행복으로 가는 것인지 지옥으로 가는 것인지

An Application for Admission

It's Jan., 2
The final date to submit an application for admission to
Korea Univ.
To enter the University even I don't have bus fare
I'm really sorry to meet Younghwak.
Lady in the market, only second of Jan. for the money
Bongyeon, Moon Kyusam in the tent store in central market
After getting applications from teacher in Headong School
What is the use of attending as an owl?
After having a shot in Myungdong with the certificate
of the graduation on hands
Grabbing a taxi with friends in droves
Sing of enjoyable life spearing the heaven
E-rah! What do I know?
Nothing will happen to me!
Let us go backward if not forward
Admission fee of political college rings 64,200 won
70,000 won my mother sent me all going out
The hard-earned money my little brother hands made
I cannot fall a sleep
Whether I head to happiness or hell

어떤 시험장에서

악몽의 하루인가?
황금의 파도는 몰아치는데
여지없이 멸시하던 인정이기에
치욕의 일기는 적어가는데
골수에 메아리친 가난이여.

At a Certain Examination Hall

The day of nightmare?
Waving
Due to the human nature of ignoring
I'm writing a dairy of disgrace
Poverty echoed in my soul.

석별

예전에는 미처 몰랐던 그 끝 앞에는
다알리아 진홍빛이 눈부시었네
철따라 숱한 꽃이 피고 지지만
다알리아는 어찌하여 피보다 진할까

오솔길 논두렁길 소고삐 잡고
향긋한 가을 정내 가슴 훈훈해
진붉은 꽃잎이 행여 임일까
기목(나무) 등 뒤에 숨어서 보았네

홀어머니는 눈물짓는 석별에 정차장
천려원정 갈 길 멀어 고개 돌렸네
두고두고 못다 한 말 가슴 태우며
되돌아 뒤돌아 산은 울어만 주네

Unwillingness to Part

In front of that garden I didn't even know that in the past
Red dahlia was brilliant
Too many flowers blossom and fall every year
But how is dahlia more red color than blood?

Holding the cow by the bridle in the narrow path and a
foot path between rice fields,
My heart become comfortably warm and in soft autumn
I doubt whether red leaves are my lover
So I saw secretly behind the trees

Station of separation where widow cry
I turned my head because I have to go far a way
Even I'd like to say a lot but I couldn't
Mcuntain promised it would cry instead of me

백한이 시집 A Collection of H. Y. Baek's Poems

고 려 달 빛
The Moon Light of Corea

·

지은이 / 백한이
펴낸이 / 김재엽
펴낸곳 / **한누리미디어**

·

100-845, 서울시 중구 을지로 2가 148-73
신화빌딩 401호
Tel / (02)2278-4513, 2268-4514
Fax / (02)2268-4524

·

등록 / 제16-467호(1993. 11. 4)

·

초판발행일 / 2004년 6월 30일

·

ⓒ 2004 Baek Han-yi Printed in KOREA

·

값 8,000원

·

E-mail/hannury2003@hanmail.net

·

※잘못된 책은 바꿔드립니다.
※저자와의 협약으로 인지는 생략합니다.

·

ISBN 89-7969-251-X 03810